KARLA MILLER

The Ring – Italian Adventures Part One

First edition

This book was professionally typeset on Reedsy.
Find out more at reedsy.com

Contents

Villa Gavaccia, Rome

Julie opened the freezer and filled her glass with ice before pouring a slug of Limoncello in and topping up with sparkling water. She held the ice-cold glass to her cheek before taking her first sip. It was only 11am but the heat was already rising off the terrace, making it uncomfortable to walk on the limestone slabs barefoot.

Outside, the sounds of laughter and splashing filled the air and Julie walked over to the French doors to watch. In the pool, Kylie and three other girls were sitting on the shoulders of four deeply tanned Italians. They were throwing a beach ball to each other with the men struggling to keep the girls steady as they lunged for the ball. There seemed to be some kind of forfeit system as two of the girls were already topless and they seemed to be ganging up on the other who still wore her bikini top – trying to make her miss the ball.

At last they succeeded as the ball flew past her and she fell, with a splash off the shoulders of her steed.

"Off, Off, Off" came the cry from the three seated girls as she surfaced and, with a carefree shrug, she untied the thin straps and threw the two scraps of black material onto the side of the pool before being lifted back onto the shoulders of her partner.

Julie sipped at her drink while she admired the pert tanned breasts with their neat, purple-brown nipples then looked down to her own. While still firm, her breasts were much larger than all the girls' in the pool and diving around without even the minimal support of her white bikini top would soon be uncomfortable. She also had to be careful with her pale skin in the unforgiving sun. Both she and Kylie had got burnt in their first week and while Kylie had quickly gone past that stage into honey tan, Julie had simply glowed red then straight back to white!

By this stage all the girls in the pool were topless and the game took on a more serious air as none of them wanted to be the first to lose their pants. Finally though, a sudden gust of wind diverted the ball away from the desperate dive of one of the girls and the ball landed in the pool, followed swiftly by the girl herself.

"Off, Off, Off" came the cry again but this time she seemed reluctant to part with her last item of clothing, shaking her head and clutching her hands in front of her bikini bottoms. The others were not to be deterred and, jumping off the shoulders of their men, they advanced towards her as she backed up against the side of the pool. Two of the girls pinned her to the side as Kylie dived under the water, emerging seconds later with the bikini bottoms in her hand, spinning them on her finger like a trophy before throwing them on the side to join the increasing pile of discarded swimwear.

However, they had not finished with their loser just yet, and two of the men quickly lifted her out of the pool so she was sitting on the edge, squealing and pretending to cover her modesty but her giggles and eyes gave the game away. Her partner in the game moved towards her and spread her knees apart. Briefly Julie could spy her full bush with deep pink lips poking through the dark hairs before his head plunged towards them blocking her view. From the gasps quickly coming from the exposed girl it was clear his tongue was working her into a frenzy.

The others were not to be ignored and Kylie and her two friends lifted themselves out of the pool to sit beside their already naked friend. On cue the men moved forward and swiftly removed the remaining bikini bottoms before joining their colleague between tanned thighs.

Each of the girls leant back to tilt their pussies up into the attending mouths and the giggles were soon replaced by sighs of pleasure. Julie continued sipping at her drink and her hand strayed down towards the front of her own bikini bottoms as she spied on the scene by the pool.

As one, the men broke away from their partners, to groans of dismay, before climbing out of the pool and their trunks. The four girls lay back on the terrace and each man knelt behind their heads and slowly fed their engorged cocks into waiting mouths. Silence fell as each girls' mouth was filled to the brim as the men rocked slowly back and forward to gently fuck them. Julie watched as Kylie moved her hands downwards to stroke at the girls' pussies either side, her fingers dipping into the soft moist flesh. Julie's own fingers were likewise probing her own flesh in time with the rocking.

Two of the men withdrew their cocks and lifted their lovers up off the hard terrace and onto a pair of padded sun loungers. Positioning the girls on their knees with their heads over the back of the lounger, the men straddled the seat and slid their still slick cocks up into them. The loungers rocked with the thrusts of the men and the squeals from girls increased.

The two other men rose from the poolside and moved over to the sun loungers before feeding rock-hard penises into the open mouths. Now each stroke from behind pushed the girls onto the cocks they were feeding on.

Kylie and Frederica were alone by the pool. Kylie spun Frederica around so that her head was by the water's edge and straddled her toned, tanned body before dipping her head downwards to lick greedily at her moist cleft. Frederica responded by using her fingers to spread Kylie wide open before lifting her mouth up in synchronisation.

Julie knew that Kylie had positioned herself exactly so that Julie could watch and, as Frederica's tongue lapped at Kylie's clit, Julie's hand moved deeper inside her bikini to bring herself off.

Suddenly, her hand was joined by another and a roughly stubbled chin pressed into her neck.

"Starting without me?" Mike purred as his fingers plunged into her, hooking forward to add pressure on her G Spot. "I thought you'd forgotten I was coming today..."

Julie wriggled backwards into Mike and felt the hard length of his cock pressing between her buttocks. Mike pulled the flimsy material covering her breasts aside, exposing her nipples and he played with them with one hand while frigging her with the other.

"Hmm, that's good - I know why I keep you." she murmured as he kissed the back of her neck and nibbled gently at her ear.

In front of them the men were rapidly reaching their climaxes as they sped up their thrusts into the girls on the sun loungers until, with a final groan one came, shooting cum over the tanned glistening back of the girl in front of him. This triggered the others to cum as well with jets of cum shooting over faces and bums. The men sank sweating to their knees as the girls giggled and kissed each other gently before rolling over onto their backs.

"Nice show, now, how about my turn" said Mike and Julie gladly turned around and sank to her knees in front of his erect penis. Her bikini top was stretched around the sides of her breasts, pushing them together and she slid Mike's cock up and down in the cleft between them. As the tip moved upwards, she licked gently at the deep pink flesh, probing the tiny vertical slit with her tongue. Mike reached behind her neck and undid the bow on the bikini halter, letting the fabric drop to her waist and freeing her breasts from the minimal hold it had given them. She bent lower and took his cock into her mouth, first just the head then gradually the full length. She had done this to Mike thousands of times but never tired of the feeling of his flesh filling her mouth and the anticipation of his orgasm.

Mike's gaze switched from his girlfriend on her knees to Kylie and Frederica by the pool. He'd already sampled Kylie's skills and knew how willing she was, but he'd not seen Frederica before and was admiring her oral skills as she brought Kylie to an orgasm. Julie was sliding his cock deeper and deeper into her mouth until her chin was bumping up against his balls and he knew it wouldn't be long before he came.

"Not yet, I need to fuck you now!" and he lifted her to her feet and bent her over the kitchen table. With a practised tug he removed her bikini pants leaving her with only the top tied around her waist. He moved her legs apart and positioned himself in front of her before pushing his cock relentlessly in.

"Jesus, yes" she cried as he thrust into her. She reached down to rub her clit while he filled her completely. Mike pushed her thighs back to give himself even greater access to her and moved back and forward making the whole table rock on its legs. He leant forward to take one breast in his mouth.

With one hand in the small of her back, Mike threaded his fingers into her hair, pulling her backwards. The sights around the pool and her mouth had already brought him close to a climax and he was soon pumping his cum into her before falling forwards onto her back, panting hard.

They stayed locked together as he softened inside her. As his subsiding cock slid out, Julie turned and licked the mixed juices from his cock and her pussy from his flesh.

"Hmm, that was fantastic – with only Kylie here I've been desperate for some cock."

"What about the guys out there?" Mike nodded towards the four men cooling off in the pool.

"They're just here for lunch and that's strictly business."

"So, it's going well then?"

"Not too bad, a bit slow to start but with Frederica, Nella and Francesca we're breaking into the local scene quite nicely. Now, I'm sure you want to meet up with Kylie again – I don't think you've met since the midsummer party."

And with that, Julie led Mike out onto the terrace to introduce everyone properly...

Julie, Rome

Julie basked in the cool air-conditioning of the hotel bar and sipped her spritz before subtly checking her watch. John was late but that was simply the way here with Rome traffic making being on-time virtually impossible for anyone.

Just then John walked into the bar looking slightly flustered (clearly the traffic had been the cause) and he looked around the bar for Julie. Of course, he wouldn't have recognised her as her hair in her photos was blonde and she was still rocking the whole redhead vibe from midsummer, so she casually raised a hand to attract his attention.

"John, lovely to meet you again, glad you could make it" Julie had quickly learned that the best way to put anyone at ease was to be totally normal about a simple business meeting between two colleagues.

After shaking hands, they sat and Julie gestured to the bar staff for two more spritzes making a mental note to stop after this one. While he brought the drinks and a small bowl of olives Julie and John chatted normal business small talk. Having her other job in IT sales meant that Julie was able to chat knowledgably about most businesses, at least for a short while, and she could tell that John was relaxing. After their aperitifs John suggested they move into the restaurant to eat – obviously he was still nervous about the whole affair – and Julie was happy to relax him.

The food was good but not stunning, hotel food rarely is, but the as the conversation flowed Julie could sense that John was relaxing. He was good-looking in that silver-fox style and she was please to notice well-trimmed, neat, fingernails which was always a good sign. They both decided to skip dessert and moved straight to coffee and Julie sensed that time had come to make her move.

"Well John, it's been great catching up, but I've an early morning so I think I'll call it a night. Here's my card, call me, soon" and she slid the business card across the table.

At first, he was confused then as he looked down he saw what was written on the card;

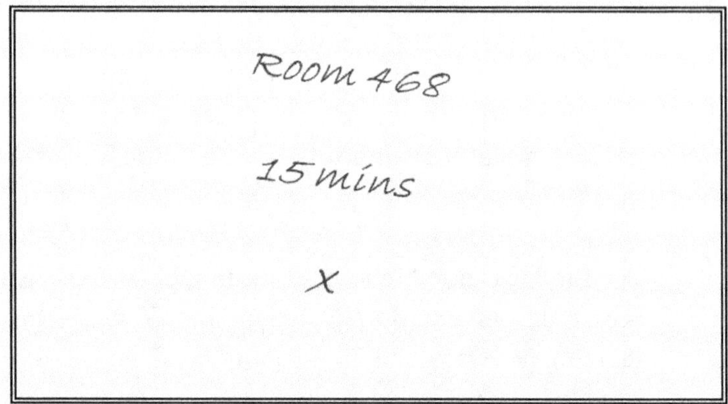

Then he smiled and slipped the card into his jacket pocket.

"Yes, it's been lovely meeting you again. I'll probably call it a night in a while." And they air kissed like two business colleagues who hadn't met for months.

Julie went up to the taking the lift and using the full-length mirror to check herself. The hair and make-up were just right, and she smoothed the tight-fitting cocktail dress over her hips. Since starting with the ring, she had become much more toned but her hips and bust still had curves in the right places. As she turned, she could check out her behind which tucked in neatly. "Damn, this dress is fantastic" she whispered to herself. "I'd fuck me in a heartbeat".

As she turned, she spotted the CCTV camera in the corner and blew a kiss to it. "Hopefully he'll enjoy that as he sits in his cubicle all night"

Entering the room, she noticed that the lights were still set just as she'd left them – her supermarket loyalty card in the slot by the door faking her door card - and the air-con set just right. Walking over to the desk she set her phone on the speaker stand to play light classical music at low volume to fill any awkward moments. She was just setting a couple of glasses and a chilled white on the table when she hear a nervous tap on the door.

"Come in, it's open"

John came through the door and his face showed he was half-expecting a PI with a camera, or his angry wife waiting for him and the relief when he saw it was just Julie in the room was palpable.

"Don't worry, we're all alone. Do you want a drink? I've got a bottle open"

"Please, that'd be great."

She poured out two glasses and handed one over.

"Cheers" and Julie sipped her wine. She sat down on the edge of the bed and crossed her legs. Her skirt slid up slightly giving John a fine sight of her stocking-clad thigh.

"Now, are you going to stand there all night or are you going to join me?"

"Sorry, you've probably guessed I haven't done this before."

"There's a first time for everything, now I don't know about you, but I think it's getting warm in here. You don't mind if I slip out of this?" and Julie stood up and unzipped her dress. She wriggled to let the material slide over her hips leaving her standing in only her panties and hold-ups.

"Now, it seems you're somewhat overdressed, do you need a hand?"

John stood and started unbuttoning his shirt as Julie loosened his belt before pulling his trousers down around his ankles. John kicked off his shoes and Julie pushed him back onto the bed so she could get rid of the trousers and the inevitable socks.

Both John and Julie were now only in their underwear and she crawled up the bed to straddle his hips, his erection strained at his boxers and pushed upwards against the lacey material of her thong. She rolled her hips in small circles, making sure his cock was massaging her clit. As she did this she cupped her breasts and gently pinched her own nipples.

Clearly the sight of Julie above him and the gentle but insistent rubbing of her pussy against his cock was making him harder and harder. The massage was making Julie wet and a damp patch formed in the material stretched over her sex. She leaned forward to kiss John, putting one hand on his shoulder with her full breasts pressing into his chest, the wiry hair added an erotic friction. Her other hand strayed down towards her knickers and she pulled the material to one side to allow her fingers to slide inside. She gasped then smothered John's mouth with her own.

She moved down John's body until she was kneeling on the floor with her face next to John's boxers. She pulled them off and his cock sprang to attention.

"Hmm, now what have we here" She purred then took his cock deep into her mouth in one swift move.

"Christ, yes" John stretched his arms above his head in ecstasy as Julie's red painted lips slid up and down his length. She tilted her head briefly to look towards him but his head was thrown back and his eyes were closed so she moved back to focus on his cock. Her hand was still stroking her clit but the thong was getting in the way of full access for her fingers, so she paused briefly to slide them off and then wrapped them around John's erection. The added friction from the lace in her hand added to his pleasure and she put her mouth just over the tip, licking and teasing it. Her free hand now had complete access to her sex and she pushed first one then two fingers into her moist opening.

Julie could sense the tightening in John so paused her wanking of his cock.

"No, don't stop"

"Patience, we've got ages"

Julie climbed back onto the bed and straddled him with her pussy over his mouth and her mouth over his cock. Her stocking-clad legs were either side of his head and his hands roamed up and down her thighs before resting on her bum. He pulled her cheeks apart, exposing her fully to his gaze before lifting his head up and burying his face into her mound, licking along her already engorged lips down towards the nub of her clit.

"Yes just there, that's..." Julie whimpered then sank her head back down to take John's cock back down her throat.

The room was filled with the sounds of licking and sucking with a background of light classics on the stereo.

John's technique was more enthusiastic than effective, but the room and mood were enough, and Julie came softly, her wetness soaking John's face.

"Hmm, now, let's see what we can do for you." And Julie lifted away from him before she swung her leg over to straddle his hips. His cock was pressed up against his belly and Julie was sitting astride it with her lips pressing down so that the head was just inline with her clit. Placing her hands on the bed by John's thighs she began to rock to and fro leaning backwards to give John an uninterrupted view of the folds of her pussy wanking his cock. Being in control gave Julie a massive turn-on and she reached over and started frigging her clit with a finger.

The sights and sensations had made John even harder and Julie lifted up then guided his penis into her cunt before lowering herself back onto his hips with his entire length filling her.

"God, that's good" he sighed "Hmm, just what I needed" Julie agreed and leant forward to kiss his chest and press the root of his cock against her clit, giving her a tingle of the pleasure to come.

Stretching upwards she began to lift and fall onto his cock while massaging her tits, both for her own pleasure and for John. This time as she sensed his tensing she continued, speeding up and slowing again to keep him on the edge of cumming until he could hold back no longer and his cock pulsed inside her as he came deep inside her cunt. As she lifted off his cum flowed out of her to puddle on his now deflating member and Julie slid down his legs and began to lap up the mix of his cum and her own juices before taking his now flaccid cock into her mouth and rolling her tongue around the soft tip.

"Hmm, my wife never does that – she dashes off to the bathroom straight away"

Julie snuggled up on his tanned shoulder, for an older man he kept himself in shape, and trailed a finger down his chest through the salt and pepper hair.

"I hope she doesn't spend ten minutes in there 'brushing her teeth' with her special electric toothbrush!"

"Ha. No that's not a problem – she just thinks sex is dirty."

"If it's not dirty then you're not doing it right is my motto!"

Julie took a sly look at John, she could tell he'd soon be asleep and the last thing she needed was him chainsawing all night next to her.

"I really am sorry, but I actually do have an early meeting tomorrow. Are you in Rome for much longer – perhaps we could meet up again?"

"I'm here for another couple of days but I've got a dinner tomorrow with my client."

"Maybe he'd like to have some fun. I can find a friend to make a four – and I don't mean for Bridge!"

"Hmm, that might just seal the deal. Can I call you?"

"Sure" Julie got up out of the bed and walked over to where her handbag was next to the table. She made sure to bend over to get out a card so her arse was directly facing John's gaze so he could take a good long look at her pussy peeking out between her thighs.

"Here's my real card" and she handed him the black cards embossed with a gold ring.

"Drop me an email and I'm sure we can help you get that contract!" (plus get another local client she thought to herself.)

Julie and Francesca

John was as good as his word and had emailed her by 11am with some details and suggestions. Julie did a quick check on LinkedIn about John's client and a little scan of his Facebook to check him out and they made arrangements for that evening.

Francesca and Julie met up at the villa and took a cab down to the restaurant where John and Giulio were going to meet them.

Julie had picked their outfits carefully, matching black dresses cut low at the back with criss-cross straps at the back. Julie could see Francesca's tattoo across her toned skin and the straps of her thong just peeking over the dress fabric.

As they walked through the restaurant to the bar they could feel the eyes of every man and many of the women focused on them. Julie was used to this attention but she could tell Francesca was nervous, so she reached over to hold her hand.

"you'll be fine babe, just follow my lead" she whispered into Francesca's ear.

Francesca squeezed her hand and kissed her gently on the cheek.

John and Giulio were at the bar and they rose as the girls arrived. Giulio blatantly scanned them up and down and his eyes paused when they reached Julie's tits. His smile told her he liked what he saw.

"Great, an old letch. Still, he's a rich, old letch so hopefully this will be worth it." She thought as she smiled and kissed both men on the cheeks.

"I've arranged a private area" said John after the greetings, "shall we go through?"

Obviously, John's deal was big because they had half the roof terrace roped off for them and two waiters just for their table.

He had ordered for them already and as they sat their first course arrived. The waiters proudly announced it as "Astice su emulsione di cipollotto bruciato e melassa d'uva" which was lobster served on spring onions with a sweet, sticky caramelised grape sauce. Julie was used to expensive meals by now but even she was amazed by this dish as the lobster flaked perfectly and the salty tang was set off by the grapes and acidity of the onions.

It was clear Giulio wasn't expecting much more of the girls than being decoration and he addressed almost all the conversation to John in a mixture of English and Italian. Julie hadn't let on that she spoke Italian so she just smiled and sipped her fantastic wine while enjoying the food. After clearing away the staters the waiters brought the main course.

"Fiore di zucca in pastella su fondo di crostacei e zafferano con caviale" was presented with a flourish that only Italian waiters can provide. The pumpkin flower was amazing but Julie was never a fan of caviar so toyed with it while keeping an ear out for any interesting business titbits.

Then a slight gasp from Francesca focused her attention back to her friend opposite. Giulio was leaning over to her and whispering in her ear. Her eyes were wide and Julie noticed that Giulio's right hand was underneath the table. Francesca nodded and slid her chair away from the table.

"Scusi" Julie gave a a questioning look and Francesca smiled.

"Could you excuse us both for a moment? Too much delicious wine" and Julie rose from the table and they walked towards the restroom together with the men's eyes firmly on their behinds. Julie heard a little Italian then loud laughter from both of them.

Once the door was closed on them Julie checked to make sure the cubicles were empty.

"You OK?"

"Yes, sure he was complementing me on the dress and mentioned he could see my thong. He asked me to take it off and put it inside my pussy"

"Oh! OK and you're cool with that?"

"yes, yes I think so. But I'll need a hand" Francesca giggled.

After they both used the cubicles (Julie hadn't had too much wine but had been drinking a lot of water) Francesca hitched up her skirt and perched on the countertop, handing Julie the still warm, silk thong. Julie moved Francesca's feet onto the counter exposing her pussy. She was neatly trimmed but still had plenty of pubes both over her mons and to the sides of her lips and the musky scent was already arousing Julie. Licking her fingers Julie stroked Francesca's already moist cunt before leaning in to lick her pussy. Francesca reached down and spread her lips wide so Julie could see her shining wet entrance. She crunched the soft silk into a cylinder and inched it inside until only a small loop of elasticated strap was visible. Finally she planted a soft kiss on her clit before standing up.

"Now" as Francesca jumped off the counter and wriggled to adjust to the unexpected feeling "It's my turn, all girls together and all that!" and she replaced Francesca on the counter and spread her legs wide.

This time Francesca knelt down to attend to Julie. She was still sporting the small ginger dyed triangle with her lower lips waxed bare and Francesca's fingers gently stroked the smooth skin before she buried her face and licked greedily.

"Didn't you have enough to eat earlier?" laughed Julie.

"Hmm" was all Francesca could say.

Julie reached either side of her thighs to spread her cunt open and Francesca stopped licking and slid Julie's thong inside until it matched her own.

Both girls straightened out their dresses and reapplied the lipstick that had, somehow, been mussed up and walked back out to the table.

The sensation of the silk inside was unique, not like any toy she had ever tried. It squeezed down to almost nothing but then expanded back as she walked.

As they sat down, Francesca whispered something into Giulio's ear who's eyes widened in shock before looking over to Julie and smiling at her.

"John, my friend, I think we have bored these ladies with too much talk of business, perhaps we should see them home safely. It would do to have them make their own way home, they'll catch cold."

John had been drinking a lot and was already slightly unfocused but he agreed and they all rose from the table.

Giulio's V Class Mercedes was waiting outside with the driver already by the rear door to guide them in.

"I wasn't expecting this" said Julie

"Were you expecting a Bentley or something?" asked Giulio? Settling in to one of the four leather captain's chairs. "This is much less likely to attract attention and, as you can see" fits four people comfortably. Julie was sitting facing forward next to Giulio with John opposite her and Fran in the fourth chair.

"Wow, this is great" said Francesca stretching out in her armchair. "This is more comfortable than my sofa at home" she giggled.

Francesca leaned back in her chair and lifted her leg up and rested her left ankle on her right knee. Her short skirt rose up exposing her naked pussy to both Julie and Giulio. The little loop of fabric sandwiched between her lips and the small mole on her labia were both clearly visible.

Julie looked over and saw a bulge rise in Giulio's trousers and she reached over to cup it with her hand.

"How long till we get to your house?" she asked.

"Not long" and moments later the Mercedes turned left and waited while the ornate gates swung open with a gentle whirr.

The car swung up to front of the house and the door slid open. John had succumbed to the booze and was gently snoring in his seat.

"It seems a shame to disturb him, I'll get Leo to take him back to his hotel" and Giulio stepped out of the Mercedes and offered a hand to Francesca who uncrossed her legs and bent slightly to climb out. Giulio didn't even pretend not to be staring down the front of her dress as she passed him then he gave his hand to Julie to help her out. Again his eyes lingered over her breasts. As they walked up the shallow steps to the door his hand cupped her bum and squeezed. She pushed back into her hand, to give him permission and he responded by circling his palm around.

The door opened in front of them as if by magic and a young maid was standing in the hallway. She didn't look at Julie or Francesca, clearly they weren't the first late night guests she'd greeted. She took Giulio's jacket and crept away as if she'd never existed. The hallway was wide and tiled in pale marble with large double doors either side and a double staircase leading up to the first floor.

"Would you care for a drink?" Giulio opened the door into the main living area. Ornate sofas were arranged in a square in the middle of the room with glazed bookcases between the windows. Expensive rugs covered the tiled floor.

"Do you live here alone?"

"No, my wife and children are away for the summer, they go to the lakes."

"Must be lonely rattling around in this place?"

"Oh, I keep myself busy, and I enjoy company"

"I bet" Francesca giggled and flopped back onto one of the sofas, her skirt riding up exposing her pussy.

Julie walked over to Giulio and placed her hands on the front of his shirt before pushing him back onto the sofa facing Francesca. She kissed him passionately, unbuttoning his shirt and running her fingers through his wiry chest hair.

"Now, take a seat and we'll have some fun" and Julie got onto her knees and crawled over to Francesca. She stopped between Francesca's legs and hitched her own skirt up to her waist so that Giulio could take a good look at her pussy, with the elastic loop peeking from her lips. She shuffled Francesca's dress up even higher and started planting soft kisses on her hairy cunt. Francesca pulled the dress off completely and massaged her own breasts in time to the kisses Julie was delivering. Julie teased the silk from inside Francesca's vagina inch by inch, using her teeth until the panties fell to the floor in a moist pile of dark silk.

Julie's fingers began probing deeper into Francesca, replacing the material with her flesh and curling them upwards to stroke the knot of nerves behind her clit causing her to jerk with the sensations.

Suddenly Julie felt large hands resting on her behind and looked back. Giulio was naked and kneeling behind her caressing her bum. She could feel his fingers kneading her soft white flesh before he cupped her sex with his hand, pressing up on her clit with his fingers and her filled pussy with the palm.

"Hmm, that's good, don't stop" and she lowered her head to Francesca's sopping wet cunt, the wetness of her arousal making her dark pubes glisten.

Giulio shuffled lower and replaced his hand with his mouth, taking Julie's thong in his teeth and pulling it out with one swift move before dropping it and refilling the space with his tongue. Julie felt a strong finger pressing up against the ring of her anus before circling around on the tender puckered flesh. The pleasure she was feeling drove her to increase the pace of her fingers inside Francesca.

"Oh yes, yes, I'm coming, I'm coming" Francesca's voice was rising as her orgasm built until she jerked almost off the sofa and clamped her legs around Julie's head.

Once the pressure from her thighs reduced, Julie lifted her face away, her lips shining with moisture. Francesca lowered herself from the sofa and crawled over to Giulio. She reached down to take his erection in her hand, sliding her manicured fingers up and down his shaft.

He rocked back onto his haunches and Julie turned around to kiss him so he could taste Francesca's juices on her lips. Francesca lowered her head to take his cock into her mouth while he was kissing Julie, his hand massaging Julie's firm breast and nipple.

The room filled with the noises of Francesca gently sucking and toying with Giulio's cock and the sighs of Julie as he stroked her breasts. Wanting more she stood astride Francesca with her hips level with his mouth. He needed no prompting and started licking greedily at her pussy, his hands reaching behind her to continue kneading her bum and pulling her onto his mouth.

Francesca had a free hand and was stroking her pussy before sliding first one then two fingers inside.

"Come, let us find somewhere more comfortable" and Giulio broke off and stood before leading them both out of the room.

He took them each by the hand and walked across the hallway

and up the stairs before leading them into the main bedroom. The room had a huge super-kingsized bed with crisp cotton sheets and a pair of chaise longues bracketed a large dressing table. A door led into either a bathroom or dressing room and the room was carpeted in a rich silver grey with matching curtains framing a full-length window.

"Now, let's enjoy this lovely bed" and Giulio slid back into the middle of the bed and beckoned them over.

Francesca climbed on to the bed and swung her leg over his head, so her pussy was over his mouth. Julie knelt on the carpet between his thighs and took his cock into her mouth, sucking on his thick hard flesh. His girth was so wide she had trouble fitting it into her mouth, but she relaxed her jaw to allow him to slide the full length into her.

Giulio was lapping greedily at Francesca's cunt. His hands on her thighs and she leant forward to give him greater access. Julie looked up and saw him slide a hand between Francesca's thighs to circle a finger around her tight puckered hole before slipping a manicured finger into her anus. Francesca squealing with the intrusion but pushed her bum back to give him deeper access to her private recesses.

Julie could taste the salty tang of pre-cum and sensed that Giulio was near so lifted away from him and slapped Francesca on the bum.

"My turn" she said, and Francesca lifted away from him.

Julie made sure Giulio moved further up the bed, so his hips were in the middle before she turned and sat astride him with her face towards his twitching cock. His tongue slid into her pussy and she lowered her mouth back onto his cock.

She could see Francesca sitting on the Chaise Longue with one leg raised pumping two fingers into herself frantically.

She felt Giulio's thumb probe her arse and slide in with the merest pause. Supporting herself on her elbows, her hands reached beneath his thighs and lifted his legs upwards. Francesca got up from the chair and placed herself at the end of the bed. Julie broke off from Giulio's cock to kiss her then took his length back into her mouth. Francesca lowered her head and suck his balls into her mouth, rolling them around. Giulio gasped at the attention of two women before plunging his tongue deeper into Julie's pussy and his thumb further into her arse.

Francesca rose and straddled his thighs and Julie gave a longing lick to the girls' lips before moving away to allow her to position herself over his cock. Julie held it by the root and Francesca used her fingers to spread her pussy open wide to allow him to enter.

Francesca lowered herself onto Giulio until he was buried to the hilt and she lent back. Julie gazed at the sight of Giulio's cock buried in the dark triangle of Francesca's pubes as she tilted her hips up and down slowly. As she lifted up, Julie could see the deeper red of her labia stretching around the base of his cock. Julie pressed her thumb onto Francesca's clit.

"Oh god, yes, more" and Julie responded by circling her thumb around and around. She could feel Francesca getting wetter and wetter. Francesca rolled forward and kissed Julie and cupped her boobs, rolling her thumbs over the already erect nipples. With Giulio lapping at her cunt and Francesca at her breasts her orgasm rose, and she convulsed with the pleasure of the twin sensations. The juices from her cunt flooded across Giulio's face as her pussy pulsed and she forced her tongue into Francesca's mouth.

She climbed off Giulio and Francesca sped up her rocking on his rock-hard cock. Julie moved down to between his legs. Her face was inches from Francesca's bum rising and falling with an ever faster rhythm, her lips stretched around his cock and slick with her juices. Julie held Francesca's cheeks and slowed the thrusting and kissed and licked them, her tongue reaching down between them towards that forbidden puckered ring of flesh.

Julie cupped his balls in her right hand and licked her left thumb before gently inserting it into Francesca's pussy alongside Giulio's cock. Francesca squealed at the unexpected intrusion and Julie felt her muscles tighten on the thumb and cock penetrating her before she began to rock up and down again. Julie's thumb was rubbing Giulio's cock giving him a gentle hand job while he was still inside Francesca.

"Ah" Francesca sighed as Julie removed her thumb and began circling it around her anus before pushing it deeply in.

Julie could feel Giulio's cock through the thin veil of flesh and gently moved her thumb in and out in opposite timing to his cock.

"Christ, yes, yes ,yes" Francesca screamed as her second orgasm of the night came upon her and she thrashed wildly on the dual penetrations of her flesh.

This combined with Julie's thumb, sent Giulio over the edge and she could feel his cock pumping sperm into Francesca in deliberate pulses.

The three of them rested in a heap on the bed with Giulio's cock softening inside Francesca. As it shrunk down it slipped out and his cum trickled out of her gaping pussy. Julie collected a pool of it in the palm of her hand and licked up half of the salty, viscous liquid then offered the rest to Francesca who lapped it up like a kitten with cream.

As their sweat cooled the three untangled themselves and burrowed under the sheets with Giulio in the middle and the two girls fell asleep on his chest...

* * *

Julie woke to sensation of a finger stroking her mons and inching downwards. It was still quite dark with the merest hint of dawn light, so she hadn't been asleep long but the finger creeping its way to her pussy was matched by a hard penis pushing against the small of her back. The finger reached the fleshy hood over her clit and rubbed and circled it as Giulio nuzzled into the back of her neck.

"Ciao bella" he whispered into her ear as his hand cupped her breast.

"hmm, it's very early" and she wriggled back into him as his prick grew harder.

"I have a flight, but I have time..."

"If you have time then so do I!" and with that Julie rolled onto her hands and knees. Giulio needed no more prompting and positioned himself behind her with his cock aligned perfectly with her cunt.

Julie looked over and saw Francesca either asleep or feigning sleep as Giulio put his hands on her hips. She reached down to take hold of his cock and guide it home as he pushed forward, filling her pussy with his flesh.

He began to thrust in and out of her with increasing speed and Julie rocked back in response. Suddenly he stopped and reached forwards to take her wrists and pull them back so he was holding them together in the small of her back. His hand was big enough to hold them both together as if they were cuffed. Julie was resting on her shoulders and her head was turned towards Francesca as she was helpless in his strong grasp.

Francesca opened her eyes and smiled – clearly, she had been pretending to be asleep.

"Ciao" she whispered and started stroking Julie's breast.

The feeling of utter helplessness was really turning Julie on and as she felt Giulio tightening inside her she was about to come herself when he came with a yell and pushed himself ever deeper, pumping sperm into her. His balls pressed against her clit and she too came with hi, the mattress muffling her screams.

Spent, he collapsed to the side of her and spooned her, his fingers still caressing her clit and the slick mingling of her juices and his cum.

Francesca was facing Julie and kissed her.

"Hmm what a way to wake up" thought Julie.

Giulio had to catch his flight so showered and dressed quickly and Julie barely had time to grab a silky gown to see him out of the room.

"Thank you for a wonderful night – I hope we will be able to see each other again" and he passed her a thick luxurious business card.

"Contact me and we can make arrangements." And with that her kissed her again and left, his driver silently waiting in the hallway to take him to the airport.

Giulio's maid had collected their clothes from the living room – the panties were beyond help so both had to go commando for breakfast, which was laid out in the huge kitchen at the rear of the house.

"So, how did you enjoy your first all-night assignment?"

"Hmm, wonderful" Francesca licked pastry crumbs from her lips. "Are they all like this?"

"Not all, but I have a feeling Giulio will become one of our regular clients" Breaking into the local business community would hugely benefit the business for all of the Ring.

●●○○○ AT&T LTE   9:47 AM   ◥ 80% ▬▭

‹ Back   **John**   Contact

Yeh, I must've had something strong to drink - I can't remember anything

No worries - We had a blast, Giulio seemed happy...

I got a message from him - you two did a great job!!!! I owe you

All part of the service. When are you next in Rome?

Not for a while. I'll be in London for a couple of months.

Then you can meet up with my friends - you know where to find us. XXX

Oh I will. X

○ iMessage   Send

●●○○○ AT&T LTE　　　10:19 AM　　　⬈ 80% ▰▯

❮ Back　　　**Julie**　　　Contact

you.

I was thinking of last night

Me too!!!!

I have a meeting arranged for some associates on my yacht. Would you and some friends like to join us and go for a trip?

Sounds fun. How many friends should I invite?

Would six be possible? We can make any arrangements and I'm sure we'll be doing business with your firm in the future

Absolutely - send me the details and we'll be there. XXX

📷　iMessage　　　　　Send

Giulio and Friends

Giulio was clearly very keen to make this party swing and his office were soon on the phone to make arrangements and draw up the very generous contracts.

On the Friday, just before lunch, two V class Mercedes drew up outside Julie's villa and the girls piled in with their luggage. They were to meet up with the yacht in the harbour and the men would be joining them after their meetings had finished.

When they reached the harbour, they transferred to a pair of golf buggies to take them to Giulio's yacht. The girls were all giggling with excitement at this adventure but when the yacht came in sight, they stared open mouthed. This was straight out of a bond movie with a deep blue hull and four brilliant white streamlined decks with smoked glass windows. They could see a spiral staircase leading up to the higher decks and the name "The Cloud" was emblazoned on the stern.

They were led aboard (after being asked to remove their heels to protect the teak decks) and they were free to explore.

Lunch was laid out on the top deck which had a bubbling spa pool and they sipped champagne and nibbled on the delicious food as the yacht pulled slowly away from the marina – apparently the men would be joining them later by motorboat.

After eating they all went down to the cabin they'd been allocated to change.

Even out to sea it was still hot with the clear blue sky sparkling off the azure sea so it was totally bikini weather.

Julie, Francesca, Kylie, Nina, Frankie and Nella lounged on the top deck and attentive (and very discrete) staff handed them drinks.

Very soon everyone was topless, even Julie who was still slightly shy about her boobs when surrounded by the other girls.

There was lots of playful banter in anticipation of the evening and everyone was helping with sun lotion – sunburn and sex don't go together very well at all.

Kylie offered to rub some onto Julie's back so she turned over and Kylie straddled her thighs before squirting lotion down Julie's spine!

"Christ, that's cold"

"I know, I stored in the ice bucket!"

The cold lotion soon warmed up under Kylie's hands as she

spread a thin layer across Julie's back. After coating her, Kylie aimed a quick slap on Julie's bum.

"Right, my turn" and they swapped places on the lounger.

Julie positioned herself a little lower on the lounger and picked up the lotion bottle. She squirted a spiral of cream into the small of Kylie's back and started massaging it round and round. Her hands slid down further until she was massaging Kylie's bum with the lotion. Kylie wriggled with pleasure as Julie's hands crept lower until they were on her thighs. She opened her legs slightly to allow Julie's fingers to brush her pussy through the thin fabric of the bikini bottoms.

Julie paused briefly to squirt more cream on Kylie's thighs

"Hmm, that's lovely – Shit, what's that!!!!"

Julie had picked up an ice cube from the bucket and pressed it onto Kylie's cunt.

Kylie tried to spin round but Julie had her legs pinned down and the harder she wriggled the more Julie pushed the ice cube deeper into the folds of her pussy lips.

The noise had attracted Nina and Frankie across from the pool and they knew exactly what to do. The three of them spun Kylie over onto her back and Nina held her down by her shoulders. Julie removed Kylie's bikini thong and held her legs down over the sides of the lounger. Frankie picked another ice cube from the bucket and let it drip ice-cold water over her belly.

She squealed and wriggled but Julie and Nina were too much for her. Frankie dropped the cube onto Kylie's belly button then picked up two more. These she started to rub over Kylie's nipples until they were rock hard, and the areoles were puckered with goosebumps.

"hmm, don't stop" she murmured, sighing under the attentions of the three.

Julie picked up another cube and rested it gently on Kylie's clit. Kylie bucked and twisted but couldn't get free from the sensations running through her body.

Julie sensed that she didn't need to hold her legs anymore and moved between Kylie's thighs to plant gentle kisses on Kylie's cunt. She took the ice cube and inserted it into Kylie's pussy.

"god, that's good, oh ,oh, ooooh"

Julie's tongue circled her clit as the cube melted inside her and trickled down to her bum. Julie spread Kylie's lips wide with her fingers and she pressed the cube deeper inside with her tongue.

"I'm cumming, I'm cumming, yeees" and Kylie came and her hips bucked up in ecstasy.

It was tempting to carry on but they knew the men would be arriving soon and they needed to get ready for the evening still it was a nice warm-up (or cool-down!)

* * *

The girls had fun getting ready for the evening ahead, trying on and sharing dresses and makeup. Their instructions had been clear, sexy but stylish and Julie had gone for a wrap-around dress in green with a tulip skirt. It allowed her to wear a bra and matching thong. Kylie had gone for a strapless cocktail dress with an above-the-knee skirt and the others had a mix of strapless and halter-neck dresses.

It was approaching 6 and the men were due to arrive any minute. The girls congregated on the rear deck and the ever-silent waiter handed out champagne flutes to them all.

Suddenly the growl of a high-power engine interrupted the chatting and as one they turned towards the sound. If the yacht was impressive then the launch approaching them was a thing of beauty. The Riva motorboat had highly polished teak decking from bow to stern with the V12 engine purring like a motorboat should. In the middle, Giulio was standing at the helm in command of the boat and his three colleagues were seated on the cream leather bench behind him.

The boat swooped to a halt behind the Cloud and two of the crew hurried to tie her up securely. Once they were moored Giulio cut the engine and the sudden silence was astounding.

The four men lithely jumped from the launch onto the swim platform before climbing the short ladder to the rear deck where they were handed glasses.

"Ladies, Gentlemen, welcome to The Cloud, may I introduce Franco, Andreas and Robert"

"Thank you Giulio this is the most amazing yacht – I like to introduce Kylie, Francesca, Nina, Frankie and Nella" As Julie mentioned their names each tilted their glass to the men and bobbed very slightly.

"Well, does everyone have a drink?" Then I suggest we move up to the main deck where I think everything should be ready for us"

With that everyone climbed the spiral staircase up to the main deck one level up.

The yacht was huge and this area was the size of a large apartment with a bar at one end and a large table laid for ten in the covered area. Leather sofas were arranged around the rest of the area and everyone was mingling and chatting animatedly.

Julie, as the head of the The Ring was standing slightly to one side making sure everyone was getting on. Kylie and Francesca were chatting to Andreas and Franco was being entertained by Frankie, Nella and Nina.

Julie noticed Giulio approaching with Robert.

"Julie, may I introduce you to Robert, Robert is over from San Francisco, we've been talking money all day and I hope you can take his mind off share options and golden handshakes."

"Pleasure to meet you Robert" and Julie extended her perfectly manicured hand to him to shake "Have you been in Rome long?"

"Not long no, I flew over on Thursday and leave on Tuesday – it's a beautiful city so I'm told, but Giulio has had me locked away in conference rooms all day today"

"Well perhaps Julie can show you some of the sights over the weekend?"

"That would be a pleasure" Julie noticed at a glance Robert's casual elegance in dark chinos and a white open-neck shirt. It was obvious Giulio was trying to impress him but that Robert had seen everything, and more, before.

"Please excuse me both – I need to speak to the captain" and Giulio left them alone.

"So, you've never been to Italy before?"

"I've been to Milan but never Rome, unfortunately most international travel is just jets, offices, hotel rooms then jets again."

"Then I'm sure I can show you some of the best sights – well away from the usual tourist traps. Do you work for Giulio in America?"

Robert laughed "No, and if Monday's meeting goes well then Giulio will actually be working for us! We're looking at buying his company to give us a presence in Italy."

"Gosh, that sounds exciting" Julie was very interested to hear about deals in the offing. She'd made quite a bit of money overhearing juicy information about deals – it was amazing how execs liked to show off yet never thought that their companion could possibly understand what they were saying. It paid Julie to pretend not to understand about business and just listen and remember."

"Not really exciting, Giulio has some interesting technology that will save us billions of dollars every year and the best way to save that money is for us to buy the company."

"Wow, I can barely get my iPhone to connect to my laptop – do you know much about them?" Playing dumb always helps!

"A little – we manage security for internet systems – you'll never belief how much information share online without knowing what they're doing"

(or on superyachts thought Julie but she smiled and sipped her champagne while lightly resting her hand on Robert's arm – boy he worked out.)

"Now you two – what are you doing being all secret?" Kylie had walked over and had clearly eyed Robert up from afar.

"Talking iPhones" they both answered simultaneously and laughed.

"Good, maybe you can get mine working I can't get any access out here in the middle of the ocean"

"That's deliberate" whispered Giulio "I've blocked all devices on the yacht – we don't want anything shared on Instagram do we!"

"Now everyone," he said tapping his glass to attract everyone's attention. "The captain's taking us a bit further from the coast, he saw a couple of photo drones earlier and wants to give us a little more privacy. Dinner is being served so if you'd like to come this way..."

Robert guided Julie over to the table and his hand drifted, not so subtly, down over her bum.

Giulio arranged for Julie to sit on Robert's right while he sat Kylie on his left. It was clear that Robert was the guest of honour for this party. Meanwhile he sat next to Francesca – obviously he was keen to continue what he had started the other night.

The food was, of course, excellent. Light and delicate yet full of flavour. The waiting staff discrete but efficient and always ready to refill glasses at the merest gesture.

Julie had been clear that they should keep clear heads at all times and was pleased to notice that the girls were good to their word and mainly pretending to sip from their glasses to avoid being topped up endlessly.

Andreas and Franco were not being any way near as restrained and they were clearly in a mood to celebrate loudly and with as much alcohol as possible. Giulio was sipping politely but if Franco and Andreas had been in a state to notice his stares toward them, they would know his views.

Robert on the other hand wasn't drinking at all. Julie had overheard him subtly ask the waiter for water in his wine glass.

Once the food was finished, the waiters cleared the tables and left the room with bottles of champagne arranged in ice buckets at the end of the room.

"Let's have some music!" and Kylie sashayed across to the bar and started scrolling through the playlists on the music system. 90s dance music filled the room and all the girls got up and started swaying to the music. Julie was going to join them, but Robert put his hand on her thigh.

"Let's just watch for a while shall well" and his hand drifted further up to the top of her leg.

The girls were enjoying putting on a show while the men sat and watched, wiggling their hips and flicking up their skirts to give a quick flash of pantie as they spun around to the music.

A slower song came on and Kylie and Nina closed up and started dancing together, swaying to the music with their hands on their partner's bum. Pretty soon Frankie and Nella were also dancing together their hands running up and down their bodies and they began kissing, tongues entwining. Julie looked over and saw that Giulio was kissing Francesca, his hand already up her skirt, fingers stroking the fabric of her thong. Francesca had already unzipped his trousers and her hand was inside stroking the growing mound.

Robert's hand was still gently rubbing Julie's thigh but he was watching the four dancers as they were swaying to the music.

Kylie reached up and unfastened Nina's dress and she wriggled to let it fall to the ground so she was only wearing her panties.

"Come, on not fair. If I'm going to be naked then you three should be too!"

Laughing the girls unzipped and unclipped their dresses and flung them into a pile in the corner.

"Shall we give these boys a little bit of a show?" giggled Nella and she led the others over to the cleared table. All four hopped up onto the table in a row facing the room.

Lying back, they lifted four shapely pairs on legs in the air and wriggled out of their panties – tossing them to the attentive men. Then, as if they'd been choreographed opened them up into interlocking "V"s. Andreas and Franco leant forward on the sofa to watch as the girls each slid a hand between their legs and began to slide a finger up and down their pussies. As they slid up and down little presses on their clits spread the sensations of pleasure through their bodies.

Nella lifted her hand up and licked her finger, sucking her juices from it before tracing circles around Kylie's nipples. Then her hand slid down Kylie to insinuate it into the soft pink folds of her cunt. One finger, then two started pumping into Kylie who responded by stretching her pussy open to allow Nella deeper access.

Nina stopped and swung herself around to kneel over Frankie before leaning down to kiss Frankie's shaved pussy. Frankie responded by reaching up to lick and suck at Nina sliding a finger inside.

Looking over, Nella watched the girls beside them and positioned Kylie over her. Kylie knew exactly what to do and nuzzled against Nella's thighs. Nella reached down and spread her bum wider to expose her pussy and little brown star of her anus to the watching men, both of whom had reached into their trousers and were wanking themselves to erections.

"What are you doing wasting those cocks over there?" and Kylie beckoned them over. The men needed no further encouragement and walked over, stripping off their clothes in the process.

Kylie and Nina each took a rampant cock and sucked them down greedily. Andreas reached over to massage Kylie's tight little tits while Franco slid two fingers deep into Nella's pussy, hooking them upward to massage her G spot.

After a few minutes of sucking the girls stopped and guided the slippery cocks between the lips of Nella and Frankie then pulled the men deep inside.

Kylie and Nina raised themselves upward to kiss Franco and Andreas while Nella and Frankie continued to suck at their pussies.

All this while Julie could feel Robert's hand on her thigh, inching ever upward until his fingers were grazing the fabric of her knickers. As they intruded under the fabric and over her moistening flesh she moved her hand onto the front of his trousers feeling his growing erection.

"would you like to join them?" she whispered into his ear.

"No, I'd prefer a little more privacy"

"I'm sure that can be arranged, come with me"

And with that she stood and led him across the room towards the cabins passing Kylie and Nina who were now on their knees with Andreas and Franco behind them plowing into them while Nella and Frankie kissed and massaged their balls.

Giulio and Francesca were no-where to be seen but Julie was sure that she would be able to look after herself and the other four were clearly going to more than enough to cope with the others.

Her explorations earlier in the day had shown her the state rooms and she could see that one was closed up and so she picked the port side one.

The room reminded her of that mock-up bedroom in Birmingham and she shivered to remember what she had done back there.

She walked into the room ahead of Robert and spun on her heels at the end of the super-king-size bed.

"Now, we have all the privacy you want – what else do you want?"

"You!" and he moved towards her locking their lips together in a passionate kiss.

His hands moved down her back caressing her bum through the taut fabric before sliding up underneath onto her bare flesh.

He spun her around so his hardening cock was pressed up against her buttocks and his hands moved to her breasts. She reached up to undo the top of her dress, exposing herself to him and he responded by massaging and tweaking her nipples. Julie wriggled her hips and the dress dropped to the floor.

"Now, aren't you a little overdressed for the occasion?" she giggled and began to unbutton his shirt.

Soon Robert was only in his boxers and Julie knelt in front of him, her mouth mere inches from the bulging cotton.

"Hmm, let's see what we have here!" and she pulled them down quickly. His penis sprang to attention, the tip brushing her lips.

Smiling, she opened her mouth and began licking the tip, savouring that salty aroma before taking his full length into her mouth, gagging slightly as it reached the back of her throat. She slid her mouth back and forward – her nose pressing into his thick dense pubes.

Robert lifted her up from her knees and kissed her again. He knelt down in front of her and pulled her thong off, burying his face into her tight slit – his tongue insinuating itself inside and pressing up on her clit.

"Christ that's amazing" and Julie wasn't lying. Robert clearly knew how to eat a vagina.

Robert pushed Julie back onto the bed and lifted her legs upwards , she responded by holding her legs at the back of her knees to lift them up and apart while tilting her hips to provide his mouth full access to every part of her.

Robert lowered his mouth and gently blew across the hood of her clit sending shivers through her body. His hands rested on the flesh of her bum and spread her sex apart. She was already wet and he moved his tongue down to taste her arousal, dipping deep into her before licking upwards.

"Aaah, that's good don't stop"

Robert responded by moving his fingers inwards and pulling her lips apart to expose the soft pink flesh to his probing tongue and lips. Robert tilted his head to the side to press Julie's labia between his lips making her gasp again before sliding a finger from each hand into her pussy. He stretched her open and slid another pair of fingers deep inside her as his tongue once again set up an insistent rhythm on her clit.

"christ, that's amazing – please, more – I need more"

Two more fingers joined until she had six fingers inside her.

Robert then began circling his thumbs around the puckered flesh surrounding her anus causing it to pulse in response. He shifted slightly to let his tongue trace a path up from that tight, forbidden hole to her stretched, wet pussy then up beyond to her clit.

"Oh My God, yes, yes yeeeees" she cried as the orgasm took hold of her body and she bucked her hips into his face.

As she lay panting on the bed Robert moved up from between her legs and kissed her breasts before kissing her mouth, allowing her to taste her own juices that were smeared all over his face.

"hmm, that was amazing"

She could feel his erection pressing against her belly and reached down to caress it with her fingertips.

"Now, what are we going to do next?"

"I have an idea" He said and moved off from her. Gently he spun her around, so her head was at the edge of the bed. He moved her down so that her head was just over the edge before straddling her. Julie stretched back, opened her mouth and allowed his cock to slide deep between her lips until it reached almost to her throat. In that position Julie could move too far so Robert gently moved his hips to start fucking her mouth. Meanwhile he leant forward to play with her already engorged pussy lips, sliding a finger deeply inside and curling it around to stroke her G Spot.

Once again, she came hard, lifting her hips to give him deeper access but her cries were stifled by the huge cock in her mouth.

Still Robert hadn't cum yet and he withdrew from her mouth before lying down next to her on the bed.

As they embraced, they could hear the squeals from the room above as the party got into full swing.

"Do you want to go back upstairs?" Julie asked?

"Hmm, maybe later but we haven't finished here have we?" and he swung her on top of him so she was straddling his hips.

Julie sat up and guided his, still erect, cock into her pussy, rocking backwards to give him a view of his flesh spearing into her.

She began to rock back and forward with her hands on his chest to balance while he massaged her breasts with his strong hands, tweaking her already erect nipples.

Her rocking increased in pace and she clenched her muscles around him, feeling every inch of his cock as it plowed into her.

Suddenly she sensed him tensing before with a roar he came inside her – pulsing time after time to fill her completely.

She sat and rested on his hips as she felt him subside and his cum trickle out from her then collapsed onto his chest, nestling her head onto his shoulder.

"That was amazing" she murmured into the fine hairs on his chest. Do you treat all the girls like that?"

"Only the special ones" and he reached over to the bottle of champagne next to the bed.

"Now, I always find that this helps me recover after earth shattering sex"...

* * *

Julie woke on Saturday morning alone in the stateroom bed. From the sound of the engines the yacht was clearly heading back to harbour. She found a robe in the bathroom and quickly freshened herself up before venturing out.

The crew had obviously been hard at work and the wreckage from the night before had been cleared away and a buffet breakfast laid out.

Helping herself to some fruit and a couple of pastries, Julie walked out to the rear deck where she found Robert at a table with his laptop and his own plates next to him.

"Morning, why did you let me sleep?"

"You looked so peaceful and I needed to get some stuff sorted so I didn't want to disturb you."

"We could have 'disturbed' each other if you'd woken me – that shower was big enough for three!"

Robert smiled "True but there were only two of us and so it would have been a waste!!!"

A waiter silently approached and Julie asked for coffee and juice.

"Do you mind?..."

"No, feel free – I just had a few emails to send. These mergers always have a few last minute things that 'no-one else in the world can deal with' except that everyone else can actually deal with them it's just they want to avoid dealing with them!"

"Sounds awful" Julie was cultivating an air of not having a clue while keeping her eyes peeled for anything valuable!

"Just dull – but profitably dull so worth it!"

The waiter came back with coffee and juice and they both nibbled away at breakfast in companionable silence.

Kylie was next up – though it looked as if she really needed another 8 hours of sleep and after grabbing some food, slunk off to a corner to leave Julie and Robert alone.

"So, what are your plans for the rest of the weekend?"

"Well I was hoping to get some time off to see the sights but my lawyers seem determined to chain me to my laptop for the whole of today at least."

"That's a shame, there are much nicer things to be chained to."

"True, very true. Look I hope I'll be finished by this evening. Can you meet me at the Baglioni for 8 and you can show me the sights?"

"Of course. You're busy and I need to have a shower and look presentable. I'll see you at 8."

And with a chaste kiss on the cheek she left Robert to his laptop and went off in search of her clothes and an unoccupied shower.

Julie

●●○○○ AT&T LTE   11:38 AM   ✈ 80% ▬▭

‹ Back   **Mike**   Contact

Today 11:30 AM

Mike, babe - I've got some cool info

Cool how?

$$$$$ cool

I'm going to WA some info to you make sure you pile in before Monday.

Don't share!!!

How reliable?

1000% trust me

OK - will do. XXXX

XXX

iMessage   Send

●●○○○ AT&T LTE　　　1:32 PM　　　◤ 80% ▰▰▱

‹ Back　　　　Mike　　　Contact

Today 4:43 PM

Wow, did you see that?

Yep - pretty cool eh?

Should we stay or leave?

I think leave (slow)

I'll get the guys to do the nec

How much???

About a half mill - maybe less
as we close down.

Wow!

Wow indeed - thks babe XXX

CU Soon

iMessage　　　　　　Send

Giulio's Party

After the rush of the merger Giulio went very quiet and Robert had returned to the states meaning life in Rome was back on a more even keel.

Julie's other job kept her busy and so Kylie took over most of the day-to-day operations and as Julie became more prominent in the business world she had to be careful what jobs she took on to avoid too much cross-over between business and pleasure.

One lunchtime she was sunbathing by the pool enjoying the last of the summer sun when a message pinged up.

●●○○○ Vodafone LTE　　2:26 PM　　　🡕 80% ▰

< Back　　　　　**Giulio**　　　　Contact

Today 1:32 PM

Ciao bella,

Ciao too - long time...

It's coming up to Fuoco Sacro and I want to host a party. Do you think you'll be able to help?

Of course - we'd love to. Sounds lovely. Let's have lunch.

📷　iMessage　　　　　　　Send

Giulio picked a restaurant just by the Spanish Steps and Julie was enjoying her second favourite pastime – people watching – as he arrived. Elegant as ever in his tailored grey suit with an unbuttoned silk shirt he kissed her on both cheeks (with only the most subtle squeeze of her bum) before sitting down at their outside table.

Almost immediately a waiter appeared with two negronis which he placed on the table with a flourish. Giulio spoke *sotto voce* to him and he nodded and went away still clutching the menus.

"?" Julie gestured

"Ah, you see they know me well here and menus aren't necessary. I've ordered Supplì and a light salad – they cook them to order – I hope that's OK?"

"Of course" and they clinked glasses and sipped while waiting for their food.

"So, I've looked up Fuoco Sacro – It's a festival of fire right?"

"yes, it comes from my birthplace we would have a huge bonfire, acrobats, fire eaters"

"of course"

"yes, and music and dancing through the night. I'd like to have a party to celebrate our merger and wanted you and your team to help."

"we'd love to - do you need us to arrange everything?"

"No, that won't be necessary – my company will be doing most of the work. We just need around 20... hosts..."

"That we can do"

"Oh, and the theme will be the Renaissance – I imagine that will be OK?"

"Indeed, it sounds amazing"

Just then the waiter appeared bearing two plates with golden fried Supplì whilst his assistant carried fresh salads and a bottle of prosecco.

As expected, the food was amazing even in its simplicity the outer shells of rice crispy with the tomato and mozzarella perfectly cooked.

Giulio had to return to the office and left Julie to her coffee and research on outfits for the party.

* * *

For the hosts Julie needed to go beyond the local members and called in Mia and Diane, Georgie couldn't make it as she was off in Jamaica with "daddy" but wished them well (and wished she was there). Julie Kylie arranged all the outfits and as Giulio's team were doing all the other arrangements there was little to be done.

Mia and Diane flew in the day before and Julie picked them up from the airport and took them back up to the villa in her new Alfa convertible – bought with some of the profits from the merger deal.

"Wow, we're definitely paying you too much!" laughed Diane "such a pity you couldn't get a decent car in Italy"

Diane and Mia didn't know that Julie could have bought a Ferrari but had decided to avoid attracting attention.

"Well I wanted to go for some wind in my hair and what better way to do it"

Neither of the girls had been to the villa before and once they'd dropped their bags off in their room "just the one darling – and none of those single beds!" Julie poured them a drink and showed them around. When they picked the place, it had been deliberately chosen to suit parties with a huge open plan living area leading out to the pool terrace.

Kylie and Francesca were sunbathing by the pool and of course were totally naked. Kylie jumped up and ran over to them hugging and kissing them all in turn.

"Mia, Diane, this is Francesca, one of our local crew and very popular with everyone!"
Francesca unfolded herself from the lounger and strolled over.

Julie could see Mia appraising her tanned body as she crossed the terrace and noticed Diane doing the same.

Francesca chastely kissed them both on the cheeks, ironic really considering her nakedness, and all five went back indoors to get drinks.

Julie opened a bottle of champagne for four of them and Kylie went for a beer and they returned to the pool.

Kylie and Francesca sprawled out on the loungers while the others sat around the table making plans for the next evening. All the outfits had been arranged and were hanging on a rail in the main room. They were all in the Italian Renaissance style with rich fabrics and low, straight necklines. Each came with a matching lacey corset.

The sun was now high in the sky and the heat was building. Mia was fanning herself.

"Sod it, it's too hot for this" and she stood up and unbuttoned her blouse before undoing her skirt and wriggling it off until she was standing there in her bra and panties.

"Well are you two going to join me or have you both become grannies all of a sudden?" and she unhooked her bra.

Julie and Diane didn't need any more encouragement and quickly followed suit until they were all topless.

"Right, who's going in?" and Diane ran and jumped straight

into the pool –emerging seconds later shaking herself. "Christ, that's cold. Come on you two."

Julie and Mia paused only to remove their panties before jumping in as well with Kylie just behind.

Kylie dived elegantly into the pool and swam underwater across to Diane before grabbing her panties and pulling them down with a swift movement. Diane squealed and wriggled as her panties were flung onto the side of the pool.

She spun round and dunked Kylie under the water and she came up spluttering and shaking the water off her like a puppy.

Soon everyone was splashing and dunking each other with the laughs and giggles filling the air.

Every so often a hand would cup a breast or bum and when two reached around Julie and gave both boobs a squeeze she wriggled backward onto the hips of her groper. One hand slid down her front and two fingers insinuated themselves between her legs. Julie leaned back and closed her eyes with a sigh.

"let's find someplace a little less wet" Mia whispered into Julie's ear.

They moved over to the side of pool and Julie lifted herself out. Mia slapped her bum as she crawled over the side.

Julie sat down on the edge of the pool with her legs wide apart, the ginger triangle of neatly trimmed pubes pointing towards the soft pink flesh.

Mia slid between her legs and began lapping at Julie's cunt. Long slow upward strokes drove her tongue into Julie's pussy and up towards her clit, her nose rubbing against the apex of Julie's pubes.

Julie clutched her boobs and began tweaking and rubbing her nipples. Mia's hands were on Julie's inner thighs, pushing her legs upwards, her fingers pulling Julie's outer lips apart to give Mia more access to Julie's pussy.

Julie throws here head back in pleasure as the waves of sensual pleasures flow up from Mia's tongue.

"God that's good, don't stop"

Then someone takes hold of her head and soft lips and an insistent tongue force her mouth apart as Francesca kisses her hard. Another hand takes over from her own, massaging her left breast and squeezing the nipple just at the edge between pleasure and pain.

The combination of hands, fingers and mouths was soon too much for Julie and she came in a screaming orgasm that echoed around the pool.

As she came down, she heard laughter and applause from Diane and Kylie who had stopped their own games to watch.

"I don't know about you lot, but after that I need a drink" and

Julie went back into the kitchen as the others draped themselves over the loungers by the pool.

. *

The night was still, hot and sultry and so everyone just pulled on their bikini bottoms and they all made dinner together and ate outside next to the pool sharing stories of clients and great and not so great sex.

"Darling, I could barely see it let alone fuck it – less of a case of is it in yet than have you got it out yet"

As it got to midnight Julie wished everyone goodnight and told them to get early nights as tomorrow was going to be busy. Then she took Kylie's hand and they went back to Julie's room. She knew that Mia and Diane had designs on Francesca and she wanted to leave the three of them to it.

Fuoco Sacro

The next morning dawned cool and the girls all got up late and padded around the villa in whatever they felt like wearing. Francesca hadn't gone home and staggered out of Mia and Diane's bedroom at about 11. Julie wandered past the room and saw the two of them still asleep, twined together in a knot of arms and legs. Mia still kept her pussy thickly furred and her dark pubes formed a deep shadow against her deeply tanned skin. Julie really wanted to dive in there but it was going to be a busy day and needed to keep her energy for tonight.

Breakfast turned into brunch and then lunch as they all woke, started to get ready and wandered around.

The rest of the team arrived through the late morning and early afternoon and the house was soon full of laughter, with English and Italian mixed in as people wandered through the rooms, checking out the dresses and picking their favourites.

Hair and makeup teams arrived just after lunch and set to work. Makeup was quite simple, but the hairstyles were very baroque and intricate with seed pearls and jewels worked into the twists and knots of hair to match the styles of the day.

By 6 everything was in a controlled frenzy, girls were running around in either full costume, nothing at all or just their corsets and the limos were expected in another hour. By some miracle everyone was just about ready when the five limos pulled up outside the villa. The drivers all displayed their best bored "I've seen it all before" attitudes as the girls divided up four into each car amid huge rustling of embroidered fabrics.

Soon the cars were pulling up outside a ruined castle – Giulio had said that it had once been owned by a Pope and it was where he kept his mistresses and their children. It was stunning even though it was half ruined with rosemary bushes growing in cracks in the walls. Large braziers were lit sending flickering lights up the limestone walls. From inside the sound of Euro Disco was filling the air in complete contrast to the ancient setting and their outfits.

They walked up the steps and through the massive gatehouse into a courtyard that had been setup as a huge ballroom. There must have been nearly 100 people there, most of them men though many had beautiful partners with them. All the women were wearing similar dresses though the men seemed to have gone with classic black tie.

Waiters were walking through the crowd handing out glasses and the girls all gladly took one.

"remember, not too much booze – I'm not holding your hair back when you're throwing up in the moat!"

Giulio spotted them and made his excuses to the group he was with and walked over.

"Bella, you are all beautiful"

"This place is amazing"

"Yes, we are full of them – too many rich houses and poor families but come through and enjoy"

In the middle of the courtyard was a huge metal frame like a climbing frame that had grown crazy. From the upper bars were long red ribbons and acrobats in bright skin-tight costumes were performing incredible feats, spinning, twirling and more. One girl was doing the splits along one of the ribbons while spinning over everyone's head. Julie looked up and noticed she wasn't wearing a costume – she was naked and covered in body paint as were the other four female acrobats. The one male was also covered in body paint but had a tiny thong on – presumably for safety reasons while wrapping himself up in the ribbons!

The performance came to an end as the acrobats spun down to the ground and took a bow from the audience – they then disappeared for a moment backstage before returning draped in scraps of chiffon that matched their bodypainted patterns and emphasised rather than hid their nakedness.

They strolled through the crowds engaging in conversations with groups and willingly accepting the inevitable groping.

"Right, everyone split up, enjoy yourselves but keep everything under control" Julie warned everyone. The risks of too many men and too much wine was always present at events like this. She knew everyone could handle themselves but there were a lot of dark corners in a castle.

* * *

Julie spotted Andreas across the room and, taking a glass from a passing waiter, walked over.

"Good evening kind sir" and she nodded towards Andreas and his group.

"Good evening Julie, lovely to see you again – may I introduce you to my colleague Paul and his partner Rachel and this is my wife, Martine"

Given the last time she had seen Andreas he had his cock deep inside Kylie, she looked carefully at Martine. She was nearly six feet tall with golden blonde hair artfully waved with ringlets and her costume was a deep red embroidered brocade cut very low at the front so there was a lot of her white lace corset already visible.

Everyone greeted Julie with a double kiss on the cheek and Julie was only half surprised to feel Martine's hand briefly stray downwards to her bum.

"Julie my darling, Andreas has told me about the consultancy services you offer – sounds fascinating"

"Yes, we have a range of skill sets on our portfolio and multi-national clients are our speciality – we have branches in most western countries."

It was clear that Martine was very aware of the type of consultancy The Ring offered but was talking in riddles in case Rachel was oblivious.

"Tell me" asked Rachel "When does the real action start?"

Ah thought Julie – she does know what's going on.

"I think about 9 Giulio does a little speech and then it's been suggested that those not interested in the after-speech activities should make a rapid departure. He's laid on coaches to take everyone back to Rome" Julie had been involved in these arrangements to make sure the girls did not approach the wrong people too early.

"Thank god for that. I was afraid I'd be stuck in this outfit all night"

Rachel's dress was in a purple material and her undercorset was cut just as low as the bodice – leaving her lightly tanned breasts visible to all.

"It is beautiful though I agree, going for a pee in one is a nightmare. I went authentic and left my knickers off to make it easier!" In fact, Julie had advised everyone to do the same.

Everyone around the room was chattering away and Julie could see that the girls had all managed to find their own little groups. The acrobats had gathered their own set of single admirers who were starting to get a bit too frisky until the sound of a knife on a glass came over the PA.

"Welcome everyone" Giulio was on a little stage in the corner with a couple of spotlights illuminating him. The sound in the courtyard died down quickly.

"Every year since I started this company we've had this annual party to celebrate our achievements and this year's achievements have been bigger than ever and so has been the party. I'd like to thank everyone who has been involved in this merger and for all the late nights spent on it. Please raise a glass to The Future"

"The Future" everyone responded and as they drank fireworks launched from the walls of the castle, bathing everyone in light and noise.

The fireworks carried on for what seemed like ages and once they finally died down Giulio returned to the stage.

"Thank you all once again. For those of you needing transport back to Rome there are coaches outside waiting for you. For those of you wanting to dance then, dance!" and the music started with a more radically dance music as the Chemical Brothers blasted out from the speakers and the lights began flashing and rotating in time with the beat. This was of course calculated to thin out the crowd to those invited to the "aftershow" The younger audience migrated to the dancefloor in the center, below where the acrobats had been and the older ones migrated to the coaches.

Julie noticed that the acrobats' bodypaint was actually UV sensitive and so they were strategically glowing under the dance lights with patterns highlighting their boobs and pussies as if they were naked apart from glowing bikinis.

Once the coaches had departed the music slowed and dancers quickly paired off. Julie noticed that Rachel and Martine were dancing together, and she joined Paul for a slow dance. She quickly felt his growing erection pressing against her.

"Would you like to move somewhere else?" She asked

"We can stay here if you'd like – Rachel would like to watch"

Julie needed no more prompting and fell to her knees in the middle of the dancefloor, unzipping his trousers and extracting his already hard cock.

She began licking the tip gently teasing him to hardness. As she looked to her left she could see one of the acrobats had lifted her leg onto the shoulder of one of the guests. His hand was cupping her sex while they kissed, his fingers probing her body.

She turned back to Paul, who was kissing Rachel, and she took his cock into her mouth, tilting her head back to look up at the pair above her. She moved her mouth back and forward, teasing and tempting him and causing him to swell in her mouth. She held his cock with her left hand, massaging the head with her lips. Her right hand strayed between her legs, lifting her skirts to reach underneath.

Rachel knelt down next to Julie and took Paul's penis from her, taking it into her own mouth. The two girls swapped it between them before sandwiching between their mouths, kissing each other across his cock.

"Shall we find somewhere a little more comfortable?"

"Let's" and Rachel stood still holding her boyfriends cock in her hand. It was clear that she still owned it and was only sharing it with Julie for the night. The three of them walked over to the side of the courtyard where padded benches had been arranged.

Paul sat down in the middle of the bench, holding his cock and rubbing it slowly.

Rachel and Julie stood in front of him facing each other. Julie held Rachel's face and kissed her – their bodies pressing together. Julie reached behind and started to unlace Rachel's dress before spinning her around to tie the cords. The dress fell to the ground leaving her just in her corset – like Julie she had decided to forego knickers and her dark bush peaked out from under the lace.

Julie bent low and pulled the fabric away from Rachel's breasts before suckling on her erect nipples.

Rachel lifted Julie's head up and kissed her hard before turning her around and unlacing her dress.

The two girls embraced, their breasts pressing together and Rachel's hand stroked Julie's pussy.

"Shall we put him out of his misery?"

"Oh, I don't think he's miserable – just frustrated!"

They laid him down along the bench before removing his shoes and trousers. Rachel straddled her boyfriend's hips and lowered herself onto his cock.

Julie swung her leg over his face and settled her pussy onto his mouth where he lapped gratefully. Julie reached forward and massaged Rachel's breasts, licking and teasing the nipples as she circled her hips over her boyfriend.

"Can I play with it too?" Julie asked.

"Of course" and Rachel leant backward exposing her clit and the root of Paul's cock for Julie.

She bent forward and licked at the intersection between Paul's cock and Rachel's pussy. She could see Rachel's muscles tensing around his penis. She lifted off and Julie took his length into her mouth, tasting Rachel's juices and sucking them off like a popsicle before directing it back into the warm wet opening. Time and again she tasted Rachel before dipping back in.

"I want your pussy" said Paul from between her thighs and she swung off him.

Rachel lay back on the bench and Julie positioned herself on top in a 69 position, her mouth right over Rachel's cunt.

Paul positioned himself behind Julie with his cock just above Rachel's mouth. She arched her neck to lubricate it with her mouth before she placed it at the entrance to Julie's cunt. Paul grabbed her hips and slid in up to the base in one smooth fast motion, pushing her mouth into Rachel's pussy.

Rachel used her hands to pull Julie's bum further apart- giving Paul more access to her while licking and sucking at his balls.

He slipped out of Julie to begin fucking his partner's mouth until he was near to coming before sliding back into Julie.

With a final thrust he came, pumping cum into Julie with hard fast thrusts. He filled her full then as he withdrew Rachel took him into her mouth to suck the final drops from his dick.

Julie's pussy pulsed, pushing his cum out so that it poured all over Rachel's face. She spun round, kissing Rachel and licking up Paul's cum like a cat with cream.

The two girls cleaned themselves up and sat either side of Paul. His hands burrowed between their legs with his fingers insinuating themselves inside. Together the three of them watched what was happening around the room.

Julie could see Kylie, also wearing just her corset, on her knees with one guy pumping into her from behind and with another cock in her mouth. Mia had teamed up with one of the acrobats and they were kneeling back to back with a circle of men fucking their mouths, already their faces were covered with cum.

Giulio and Francesca were on a nearby bench, Francesca was on her back with her legs in the air and Giulio was naked on top of her. Andreas was standing by her side, feeding his cock into her mouth. Suddenly he withdrew and pumped his cum all over her breasts.

All around them, couples and groups were fucking - a few men were in the corner holding drinks in one hand and wanking with the other.

"If you'll excuse me, I need to speak to someone – Rachel, please call me" and Julie walked over to the men.

"Gentlemen, do you need a hand with anything?"

The men laughed.

"Come with me" and Julie took two of the men over to a quiet corner of the room. "Now, you seem to be slightly overdressed".

They needed no further encouragement and quickly stripped naked. Their firm, tanned bodies gleamed in lights from the dancefloor.

"That's better, now which of you wants to fuck me first?" and she knelt up on the bench and wiggled her bum. The guys knew exactly what to do and soon she had a cock deep in her pussy and another in her mouth. The two men set up a steady rhythm with her body being pushed forward and back between the two rampant pillars of flesh.

Suddenly they both withdrew and switched. The penis at her face was glistening with her own wetness before they once again plunged into her. She closed her eyes and lost herself in the moment as hands held her head. She felt a thumb press up against her anus and allowed it to enter, the pressure from the finger against the thin wall of flesh pushed her over the edge into her first orgasm of the night. She would have screamed in joy but her mouth was suddenly filled with cum which she swallowed down greedily. The softening cock was soon replaced by another from the group of men which she gladly took deep to the back of her throat. She felt the warm pulsing of more cum in her pussy. The cock and thumb withdrew and a fourth replaced it. Hands rested on her back to steady her as a faster thrusting replaced the slow steady rhythm. After only a few minutes he withdrew and splashed cum across her back – the sight of which drove the penis in her mouth into filling her again with thick salty sperm.

The four men lifted her exhausted body up and put one of their jackets over her shoulders while one fetched her champagne.

She leant back and relaxed as one lowered his face between her thighs and kissed and licked her pussy clean. They could tell she was too tired, so each kissed her on the cheeks and left her to rest and recover.

Julie spent a few minutes watching the orgy going on around her. When she had got the strength back in her legs she walked around the room, keeping track of all the girls and making sure everyone was OK.

In a side room Diane was centre stage. One of the guests was seated on a chair in the middle of the room which was dark except for a single spotlight. Diane was still in her white lacy corset and she was straddling him with his cock inside her.

Behind the couple was Andreas and he had slid his cock deep into her ass so that she was pinned between the two of them. Andreas was moving in and out gently and Julie was transfixed by the sight of the three of them moving in sync and the look on Diane's face.

She walked over and faced Diane, kissed her, and whispered "You OK?"

"Oh god yes – you need to do this it's amazing"

Julie looked around the room to see couples all watching the threesome in the middle. Paul and Rachel were in the room. Paul was naked and Rachel was sitting astride him, his fingers deep inside her as they watched the scene.

"Would you like to join me?" she asked, cupping Rachel's breast in one hand.

"hmm, what do you have in mind?" Rachel reached down and stroked a finger through Julie's pubes before tasting her.

"Come with me" and she led them both to the middle of the room next to Diane and the two men.

"Take a seat" as she guided Paul onto a chair and she knelt in front to take his cock into her mouth -sucking it briefly before asking Rachel.

"Rachel, get some of that lube from over there" and she returned to the cock in front of her.

She raised her bum into the air and Rachel stood astride her hips facing the audience. She dribbled the lube into the crack between Julie's buttocks, she flinched as the cold lube slid downwards followed by Rachel's fingers as she massaged it around Julie's anus, sliding first one then another finger inside.

Once Julie felt her arse was sufficiently relaxed she stood up, turned around and then slowly lowered herself towards Paul's cock.

Rachel helped guide her lover's cock into Julie's anus and Julie sank onto Paul's lap. She paused and leant back to rest on Paul's chest.

Rachel sank down between Paul's legs and began stroking Julie's pussy, spreading her lips wide and licking at her clit. The feeling of her back passage filled with Paul's cock while Rachel was licking and kissing her pussy was incredible. She lifted herself upwards then lowered herself back down to control the fucking of her arse.

Soon she was approaching orgasm and could not take the strain on her legs so sat back onto Paul's lap. Paul took her legs and lifted them up exposing her anus and cunt to the watchers.

Rachel moved away briefly and returned with a small dildo about 5 inches long and shaped like a penis with ribbed veins along its length.

She licked and sucked on it until it was wet then pressed it up against Julie's pussy before sliding it in.

"Oh christ, that's amazing" Julie screamed as Rachel started pumping the dildo in and out. The ribbing rubbed the thin wall of flesh between her cunt and arse and took Julie over the edge into her orgasm.

She lay panting on top of Paul still feeling his cock hard inside her but she didn't have the strength to fuck him any more.

Rachel lifted Julie off and sat on Paul's lap. Julie crouched in front of the pair and applied lube to Rachel then guided Paul's cock into his lover until she was impaled on him just like Julie had been. He too took Rachels legs and lifted them up and back and started to buck his hips and fuck her.

Julie curled two fingers inside Rachel and began to finger fuck her pussy.

Soon she could see Paul's balls tighten then pump Rachel's arse full of cum and she sped up her fingers until Rachel came as well.

She stood and turned to show the watchers the cum trickling

from her arse onto the floor to loud applause.

Rachel and Julie embraced and left the room together to find champagne...

The Afterparty

•••• ○ Vodafone LTE   12:17 PM   85%

‹ Back   Rachel   Contact

Today 4:01 PM

Hi Julie, Great night last night - we had a blast

hmm it was - glad you both enjoyed

Oh yeah!

I heard a hint that you do this stuff more than just for fun?

Well fun and more is better than just fun!!!!

I'm always up for more (as you could tell!) tell me more...

Let's meet - Lunch tomorrow? My place?

XXXX

iMessage   Send

●●●○○ Vodafone LTE   12:27 PM   67%
Back   Mike   Contact
Hi Babe, Missed you last night
Missed you too - fun???
Oh yeah - loads of it
By it you mean?...
Too right - you know that thing we've never done?
Hmm, I think so - tell me more
Well Diane persuaded me and it was a maz ing!!!
Now that is something I need to see!
Oh you will babe - you will XXXX
iMessage   Send

•••••○ Vodafone LTE   4:10 PM   85%
‹ Back   Giulio   Contact

Today 4:01 PM

Bella, The party was amazing - thank you all our best ever

Giulio, we had a blast. We must meet again.

Yes of course, I heard about your show maybe we can talk about that!

Oh yes, that! well maybe we can repeat!

We have some clients from the US coming across next month.

Send us the dates and we can sort something for you I'm sure.

iMessage   Send

The story continues...